THE FORCE AWAKENS: VOLUME 6

Luke Skywalker has vanished. In his absence, the sinister First Order has risen from the ashes of the Empire and will not rest until the last Jedi has been destroyed. The First Order and the Resistance are desperately searching for a map leading directly to Skywalker that is hidden inside the droid BB-8.

Finn, a former stormtrooper, and Rey, a young scavenger, become allies with the Resistance droid carrying the incomplete map to the missing Jedi while befriending Rebellion heroes Han Solo and Chewbacca. However, when trying to return BB-8 to the Resistance, Rey is captured by Kylo Ren and taken to Starkiller – the home base of the First Order.

Upon attempting a rescue mission, Finn and Han infiltrate the First Order base, only to find Rey has escaped on her own. But when Han comes face-to-face with Kylo Ren, his son betrays him once and for all...

CHUCK WENDIG
Writer

LUKE ROSS
Artist

FRANK MARTIN & GURU eFX
Colorists

VC's CLAYTON COWLES
Letterer

PAOLO RIVERA
Cover Artist

HEATHER ANTOS
Editor

JORDAN D. WHITE
Supervising Editor

C.B. CEBULSKI
Executive Editor

AXEL ALONSO
Editor In Chief

JOE QUESADA
Chief Creative Officer

DAN BUCKLEY
Publisher

Based on the screenplay by
LAWRENCE KASDAN & J.J. ABRAMS
and
MICHAEL ARNDT

For Lucasfilm:
Creative Director **MICHAEL SIGLAIN**
Senior Editor **FRANK PARISI**
Lucasfilm Story Group **RAYNE ROBERTS, PABLO HIDALGO, LELAND CHEE, MATT MARTIN**

ABDO
Spotlight

ABDOPUBLISHING.COM

Reinforced library bound edition published in 2018 by Spotlight,
a division of ABDO, PO Box 398166, Minneapolis, Minnesota 55439.
Spotlight produces high-quality reinforced library bound editions for
schools and libraries. Published by agreement with Marvel Characters, Inc.

Printed in the United States of America, North Mankato, Minnesota.
042017
092017

 THIS BOOK CONTAINS
RECYCLED MATERIALS

marvelkids.com

STAR WARS © & TM 2017 LUCASFILM LTD.

PUBLISHER'S CATALOGING IN PUBLICATION DATA

Names: Wendig, Chuck, author. | Ross, Luke ; Martin, Frank ; Laming, Marc,
   illustrators.
Title: The force awakens / writer: Chuck Wendig ; art: Luke Ross ; Frank Martin ;
   Marc Laming.
Description: Reinforced library bound edition. | Minneapolis, Minnesota : Spotlight,
   2018. | Series: Star wars : the force awakens | Volumes 1, 2, 4, 5, and 6 written
   by Chuck Wendig ; illustrated by Luke Ross & Frank Martin. | Volume 3 written
   by Chuck Wendig ; illustrated by Marc Laming & Frank Martin.
Summary: Three decades after the Rebel Alliance destroyed the Galactic Empire, a
   stirring in the Force brings young scavenger Rey, deserting Stormtrooper Finn,
   ace pilot Poe, and dark apprentice Kylo Ren's lives crashing together as the
   awakening begins.
Identifiers: LCCN 2016961930 | ISBN 9781532140228 (volume 1) | ISBN
   9781532140235 (volume 2) | ISBN 9781532140242 (volume 3) | ISBN
   9781532140259 (volume 4) | ISBN 9781532140266 (volume 5) | ISBN
   9781532140273 (volume 6)
Subjects: LCSH: Star Wars fiction--Comic book, strips, etc.--Juvenile fiction. |
   Space warfare--Juvenile fiction. | Adventure and adventurers--Juvenile fiction. |
   Graphic novels--Juvenile fiction.
Classification: DDC 741.5--dc23
LC record available at https://lccn.loc.gov/2016961930

Spotlight

A Division of ABDO
abdopublishing.com

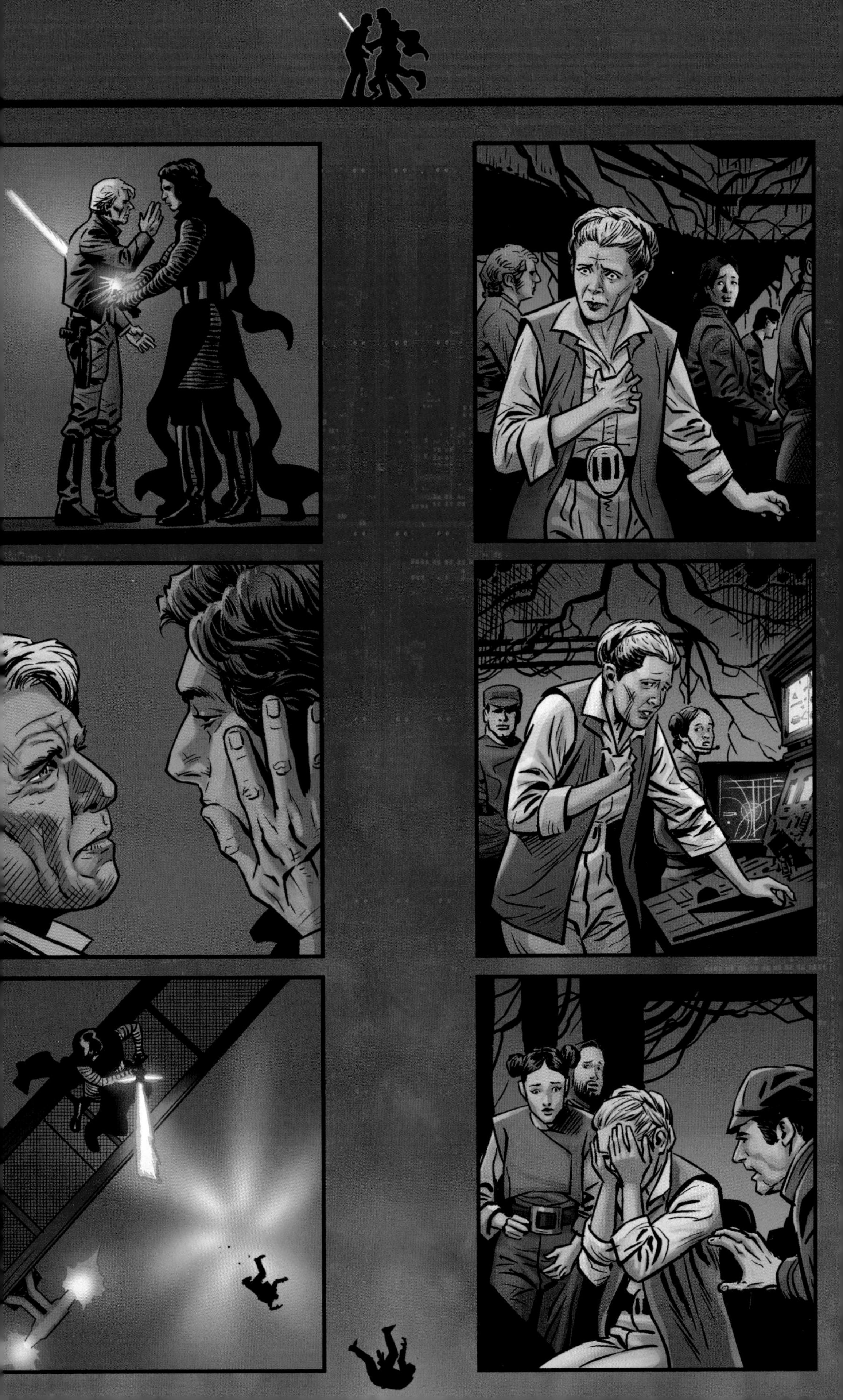

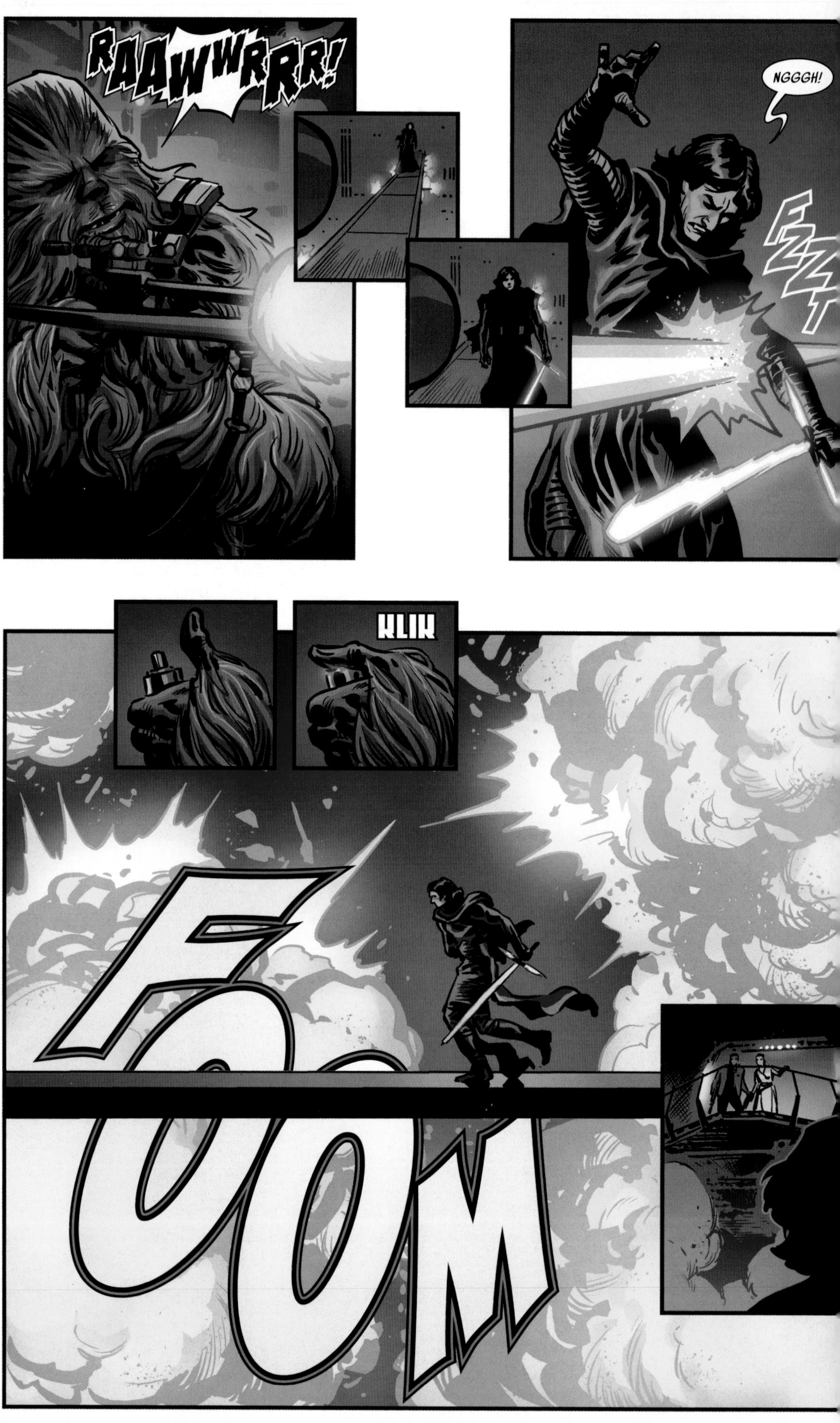
RAAWWRRR!
NGGGH!
FZZT
KLIK
FOOM

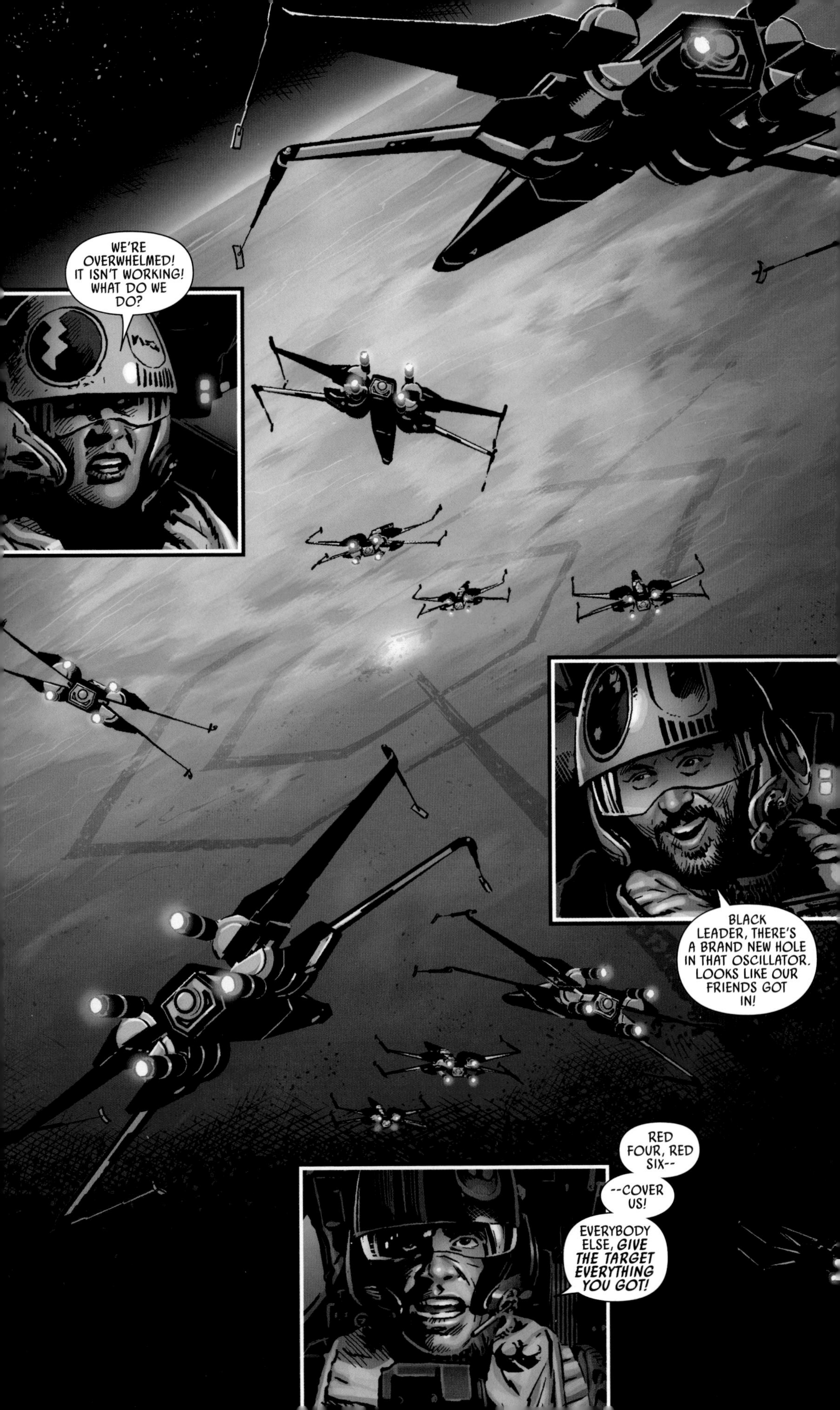
WE'RE OVERWHELMED! IT ISN'T WORKING! WHAT DO WE DO?
BLACK LEADER, THERE'S A BRAND NEW HOLE IN THAT OSCILLATOR. LOOKS LIKE OUR FRIENDS GOT IN!
RED FOUR, RED SIX--
--COVER US!
EVERYBODY ELSE, *GIVE THE TARGET EVERYTHING YOU GOT!*

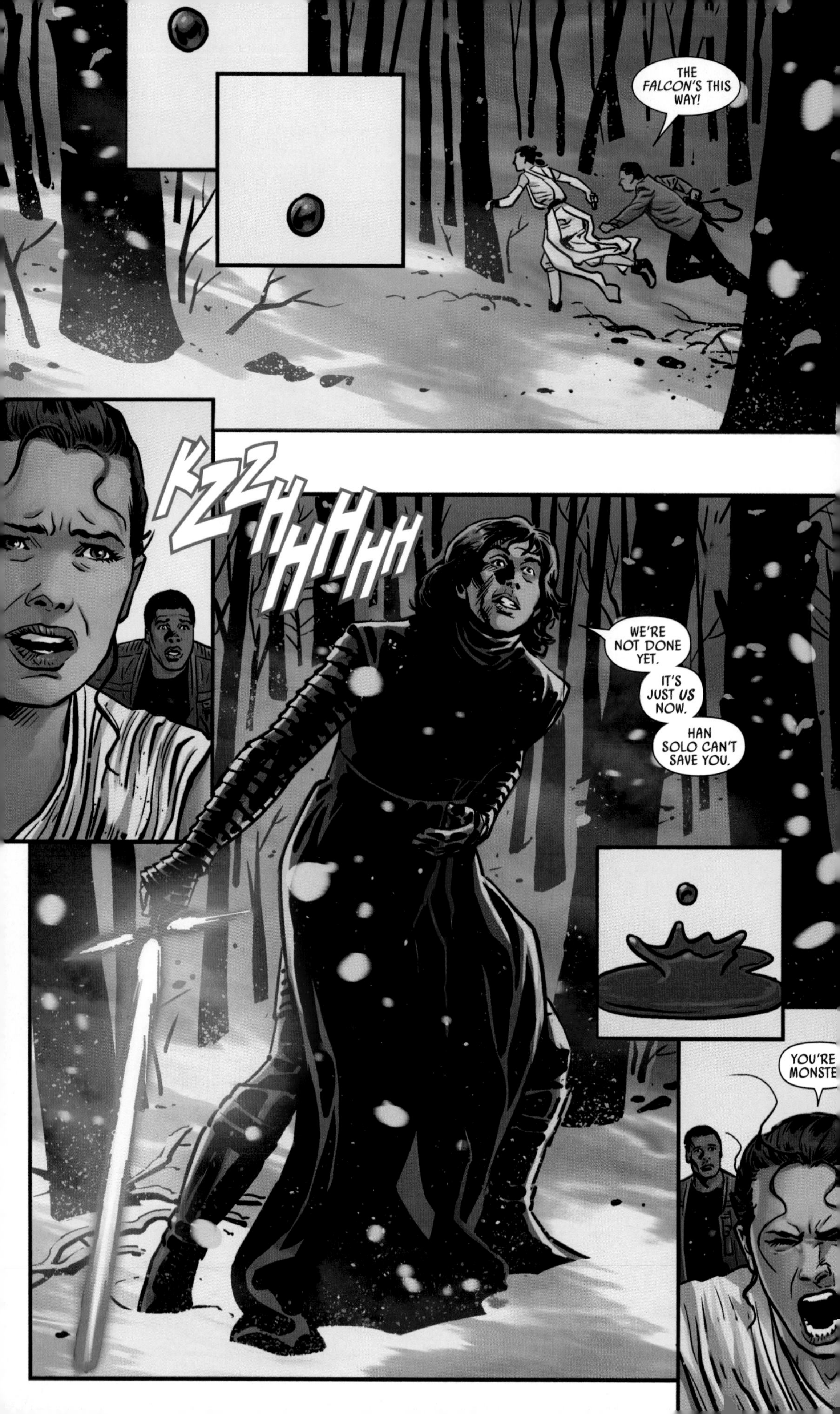
THE FALCON'S THIS WAY!
KZZHHHHHH
WE'RE NOT DONE YET.
IT'S JUST US NOW.
HAN SOLO CAN'T SAVE YOU.
YOU'RE

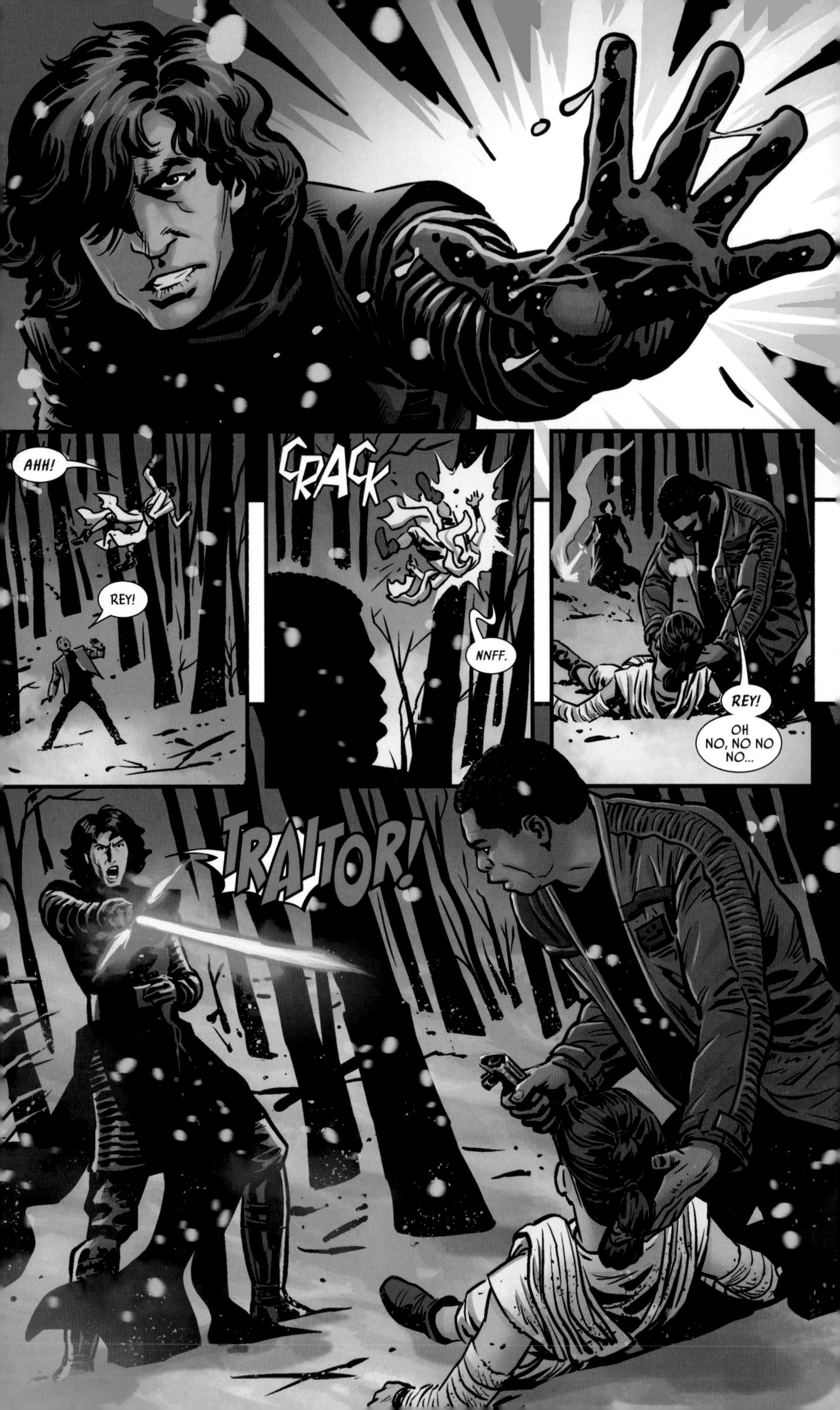
AHH!
REY!
CRACK
NNFF.
REY!
OH NO, NO NO NO...
TRAITOR!

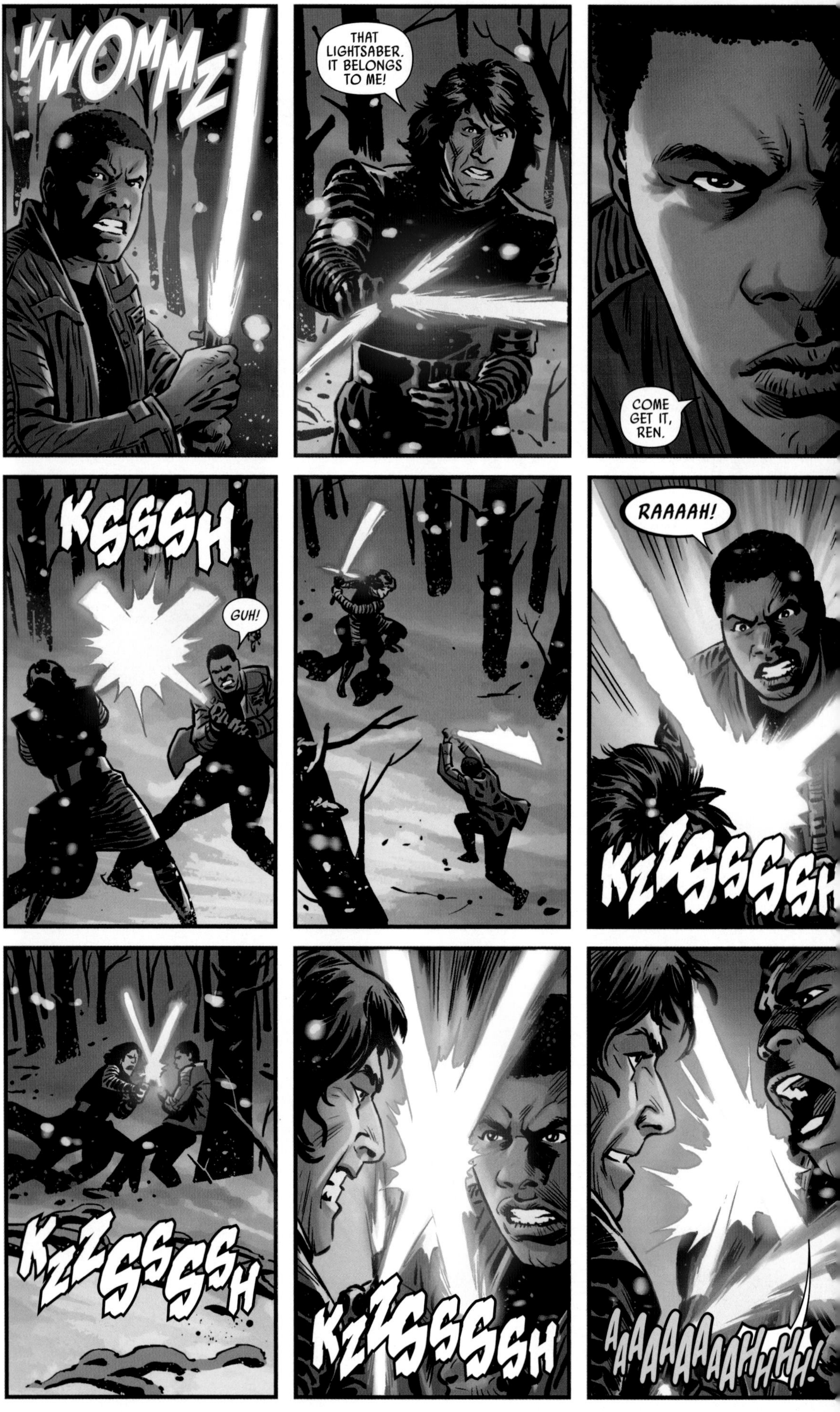
VWOMMZ
THAT LIGHTSABER. IT BELONGS TO ME!
COME GET IT, REN.
KSSSH
GUH!
RAAAAH!
KZZSSSSH
KZZSSSSSH
KZZSSSSSH
AAAAAAAAAHHHH!

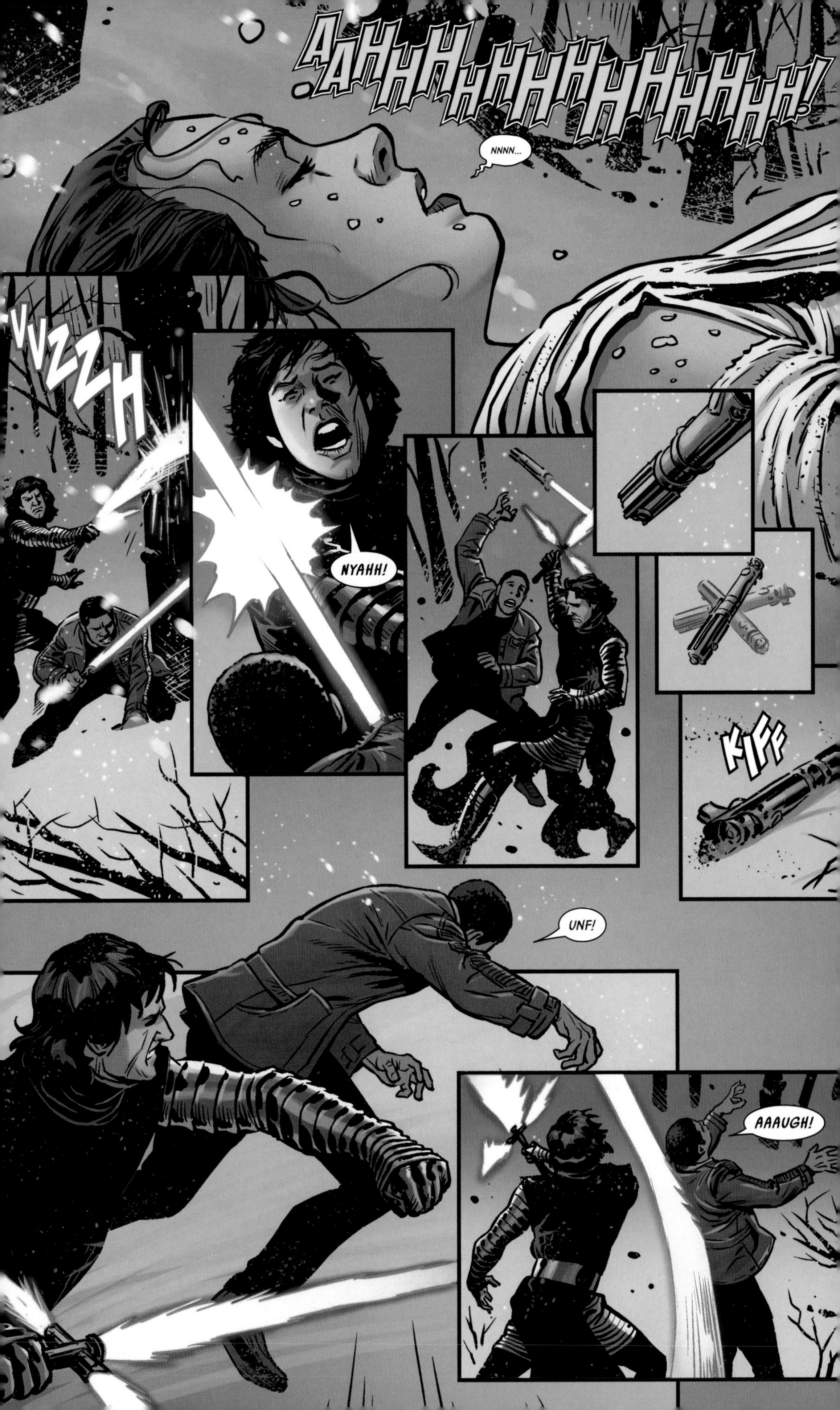
AAHHHHHHHHHHHHHHH!
NNNN...
VVZZZH
NYAHH!
KIFF
UNF!
AAAUGH!

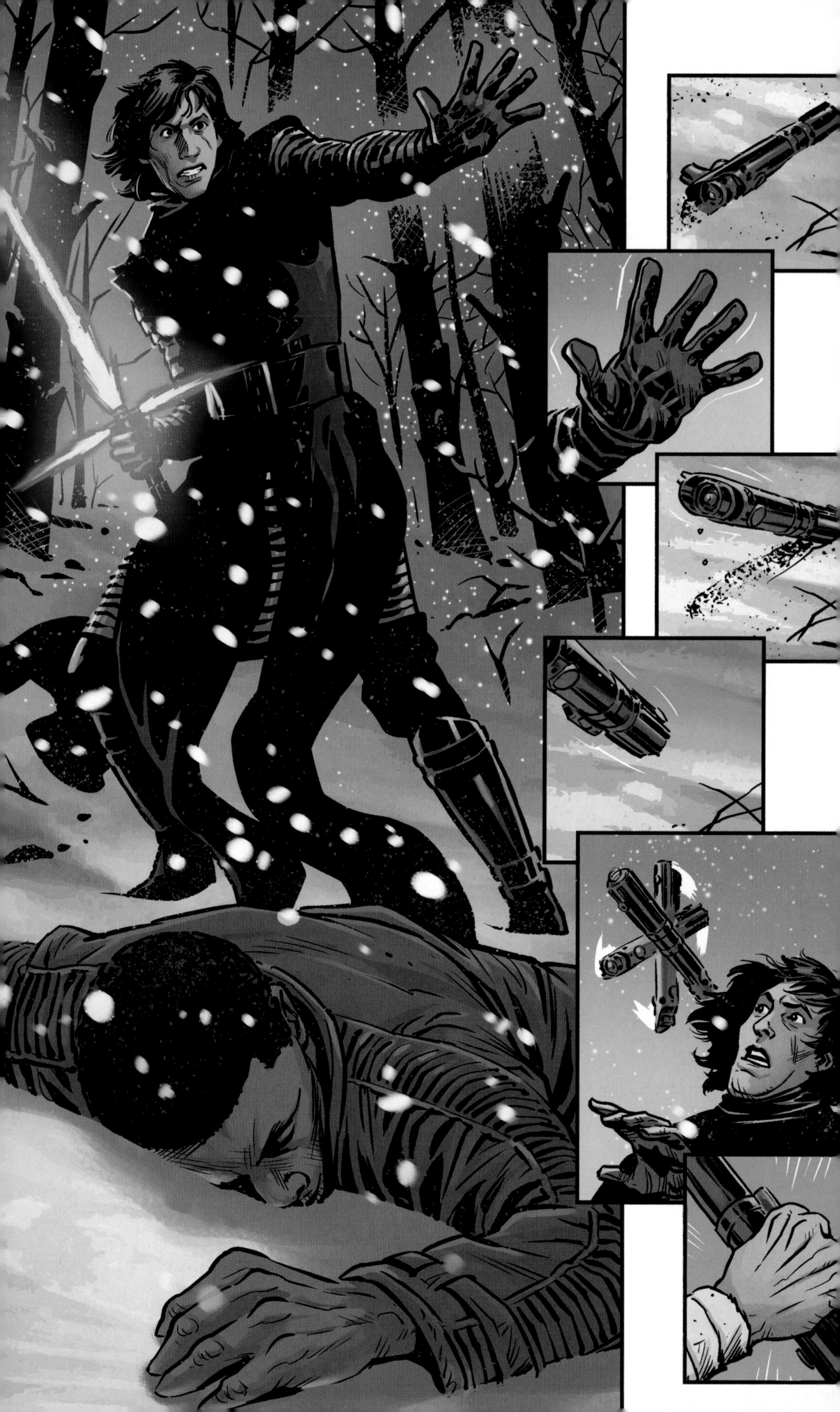

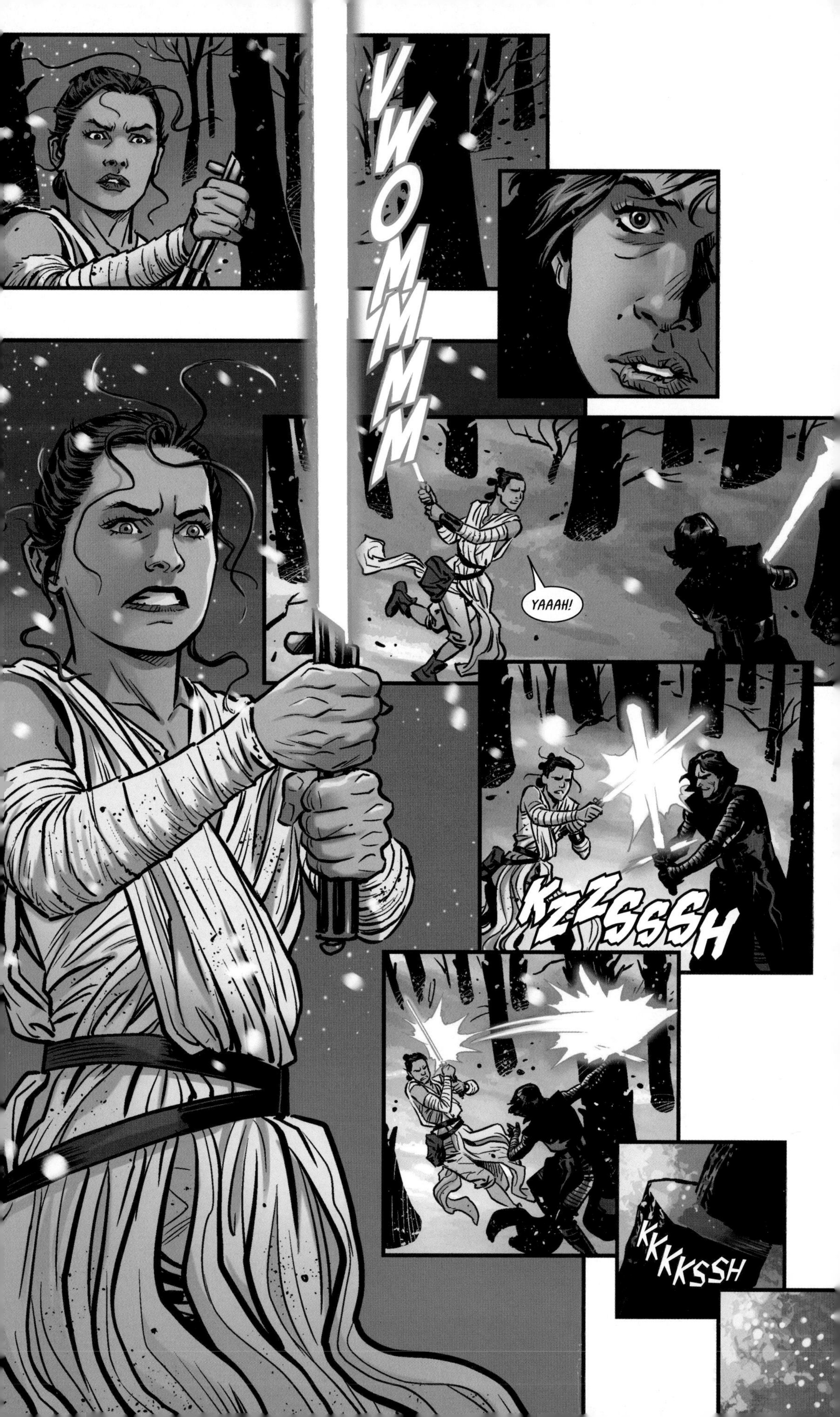
VWOMMMM
YAAAH!
KZZSSSSH
KKKKSSH

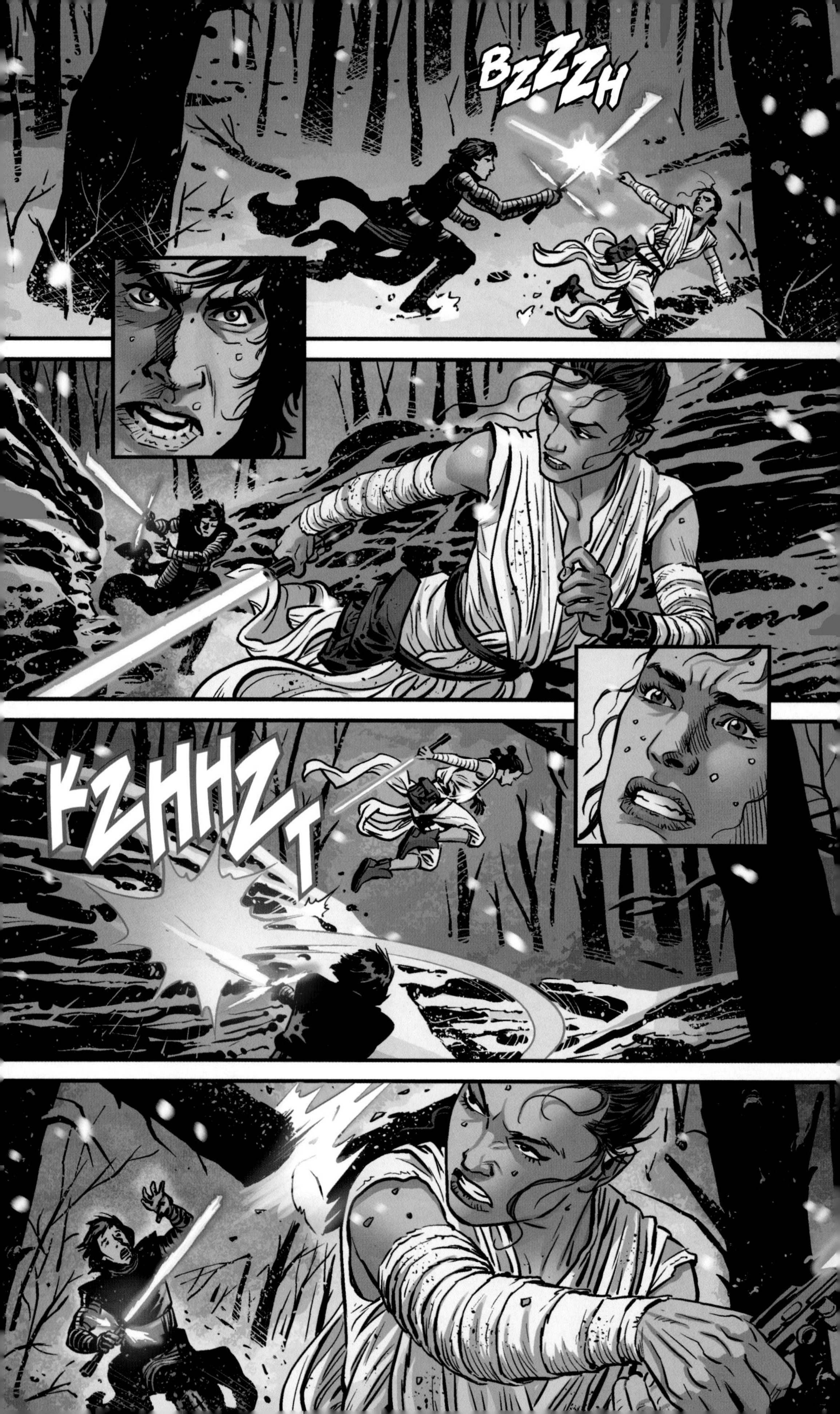
BZZZH
KZHHZT

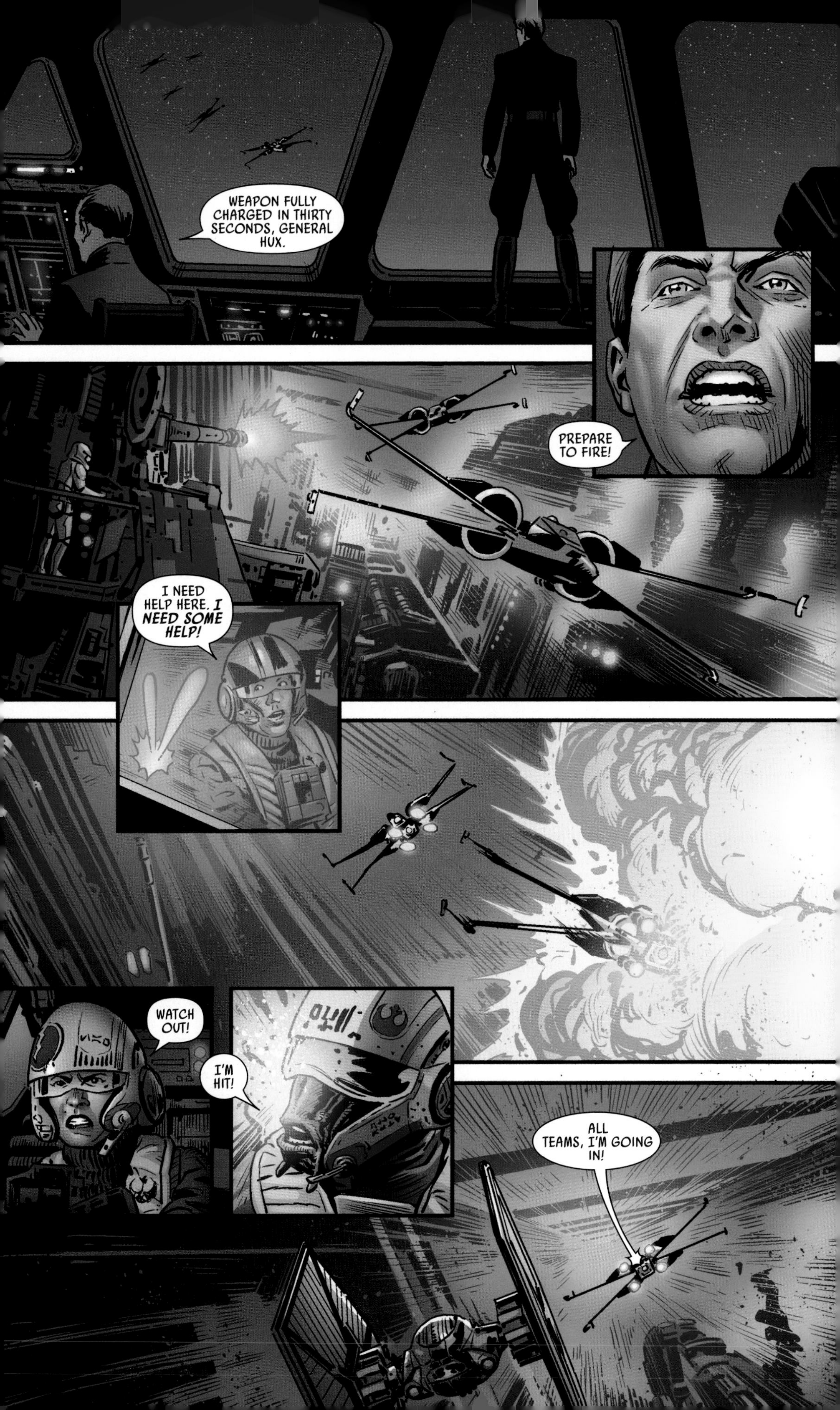
WEAPON FULLY CHARGED IN THIRTY SECONDS, GENERAL HUX.
PREPARE TO FIRE!
I NEED HELP HERE. *I NEED SOME HELP!*
WATCH OUT!
I'M HIT!
ALL TEAMS, I'M GOING IN!

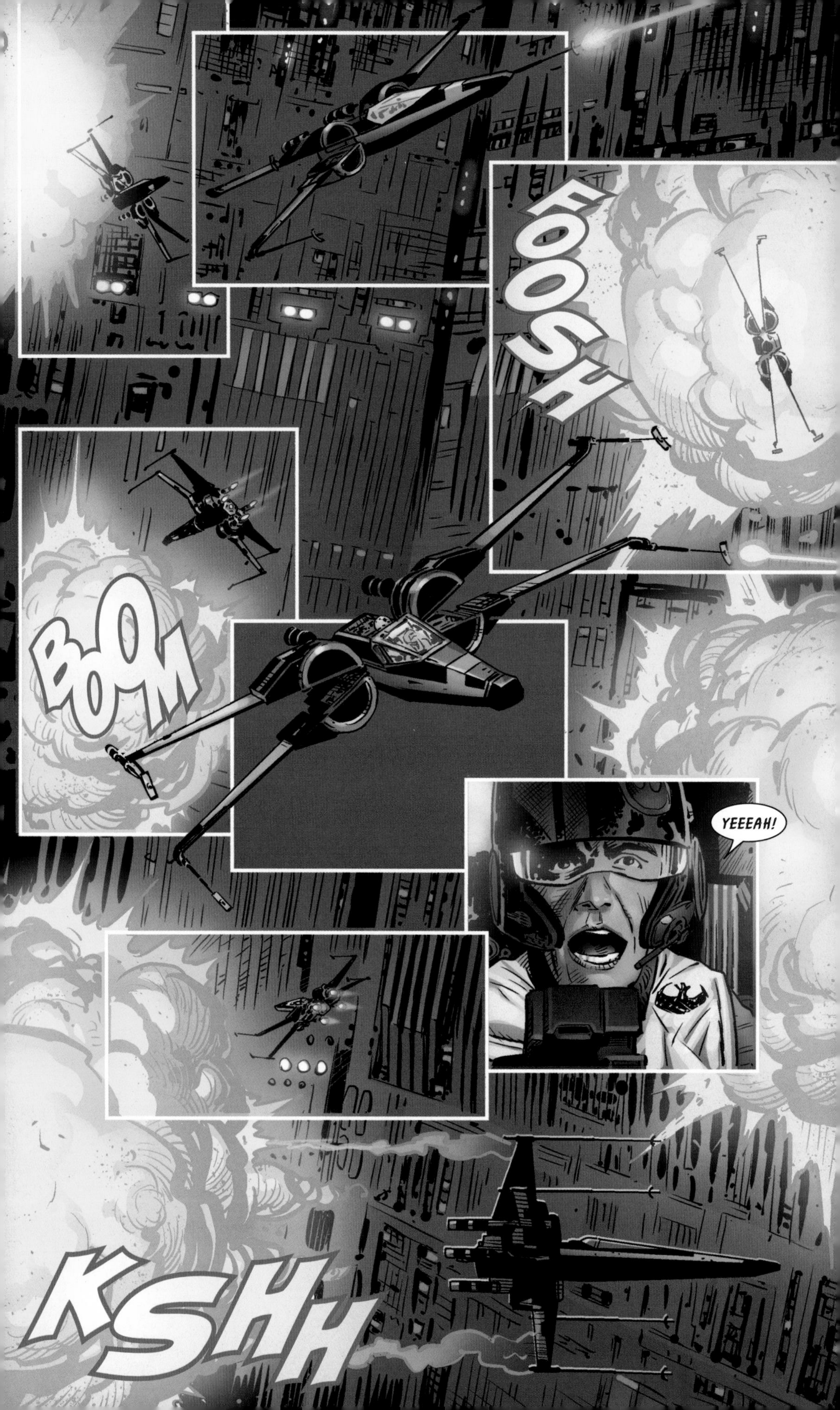

FOOSH
BOOM
YEEEAH!
KSHH

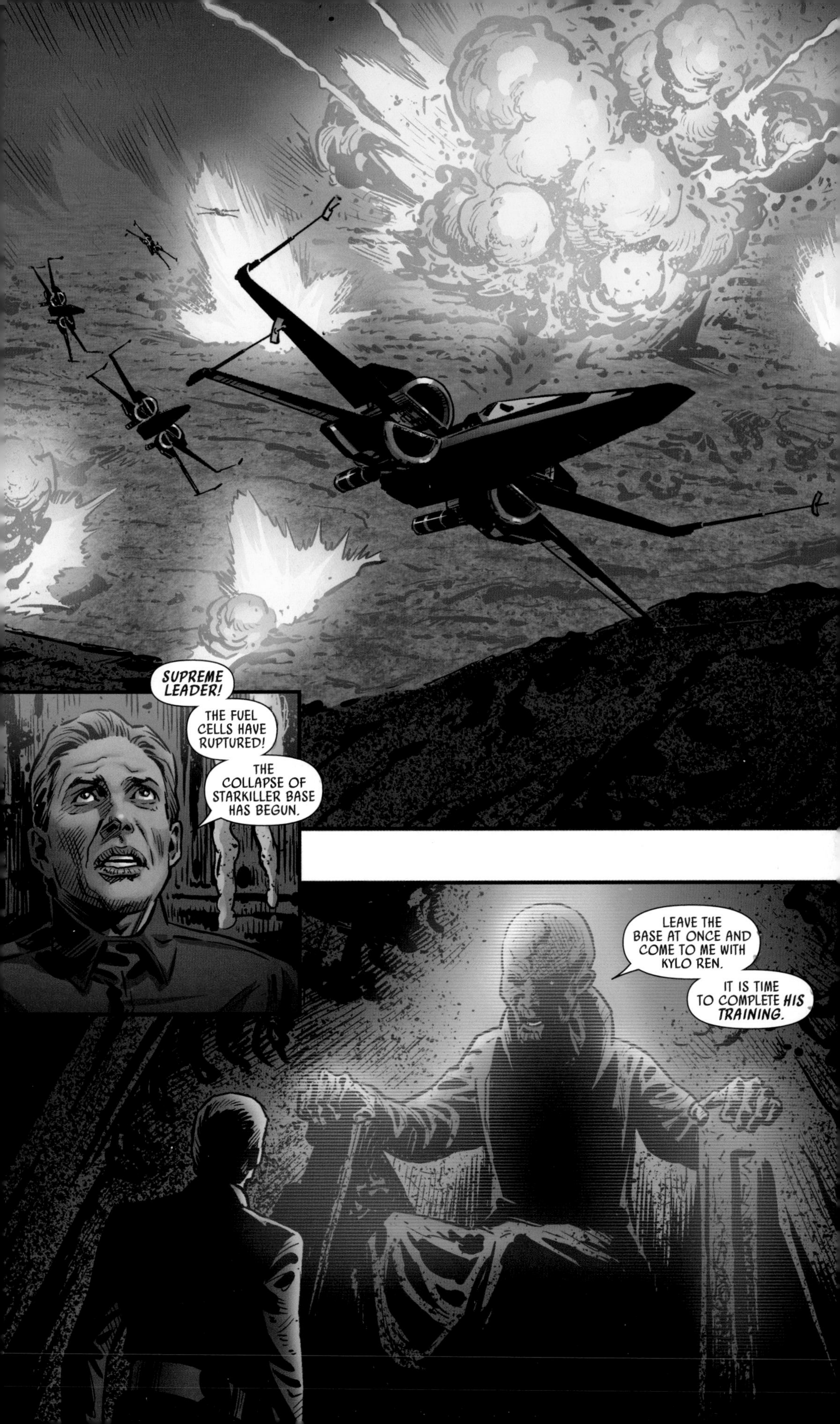
SUPREME LEADER!
THE FUEL CELLS HAVE RUPTURED!
THE COLLAPSE OF STARKILLER BASE HAS BEGUN.
LEAVE THE BASE AT ONCE AND COME TO ME WITH KYLO REN.
IT IS TIME TO COMPLETE HIS TRAINING.

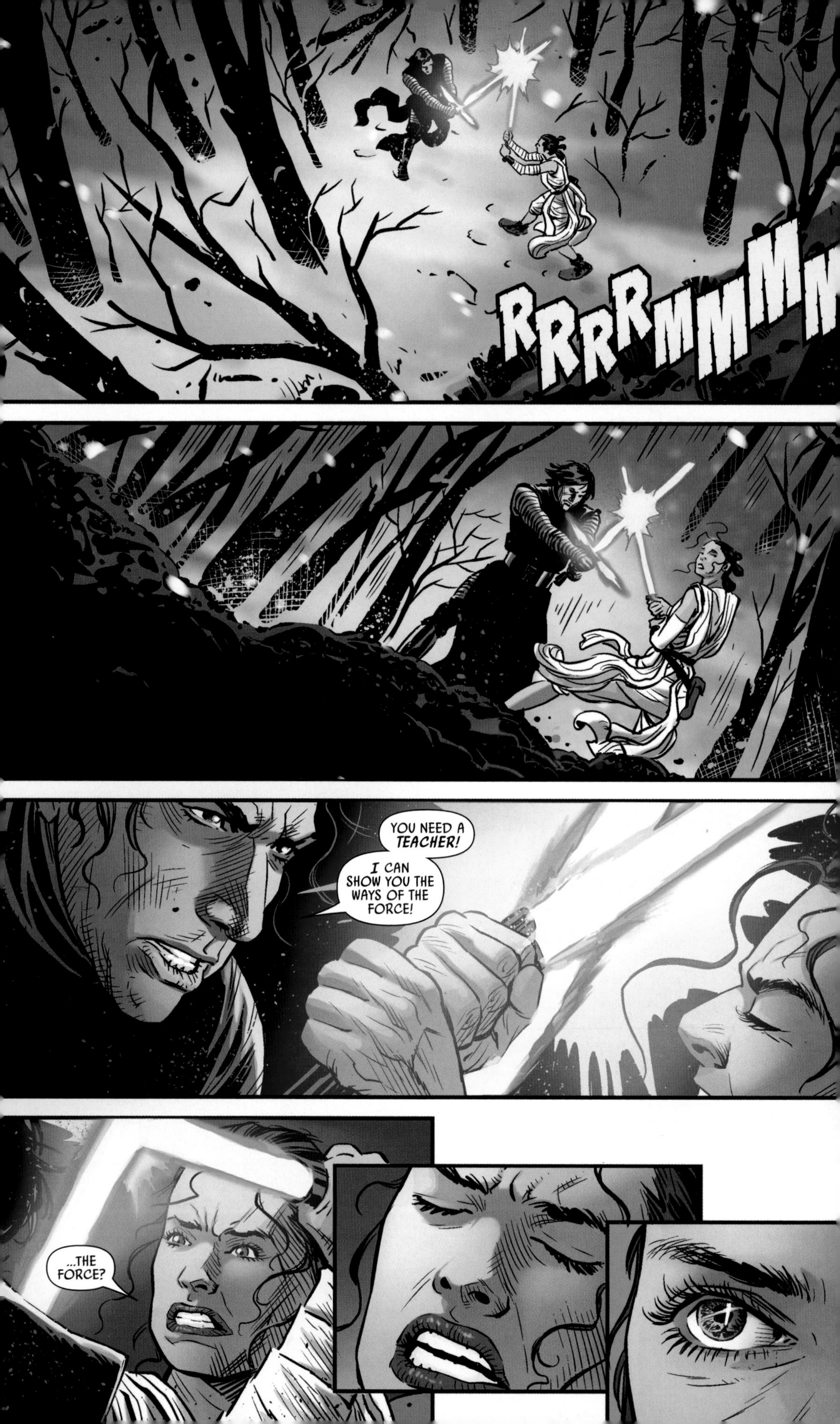
RRRRMMMMM
YOU NEED A *TEACHER!*
I CAN SHOW YOU THE WAYS OF THE FORCE!
...THE FORCE?

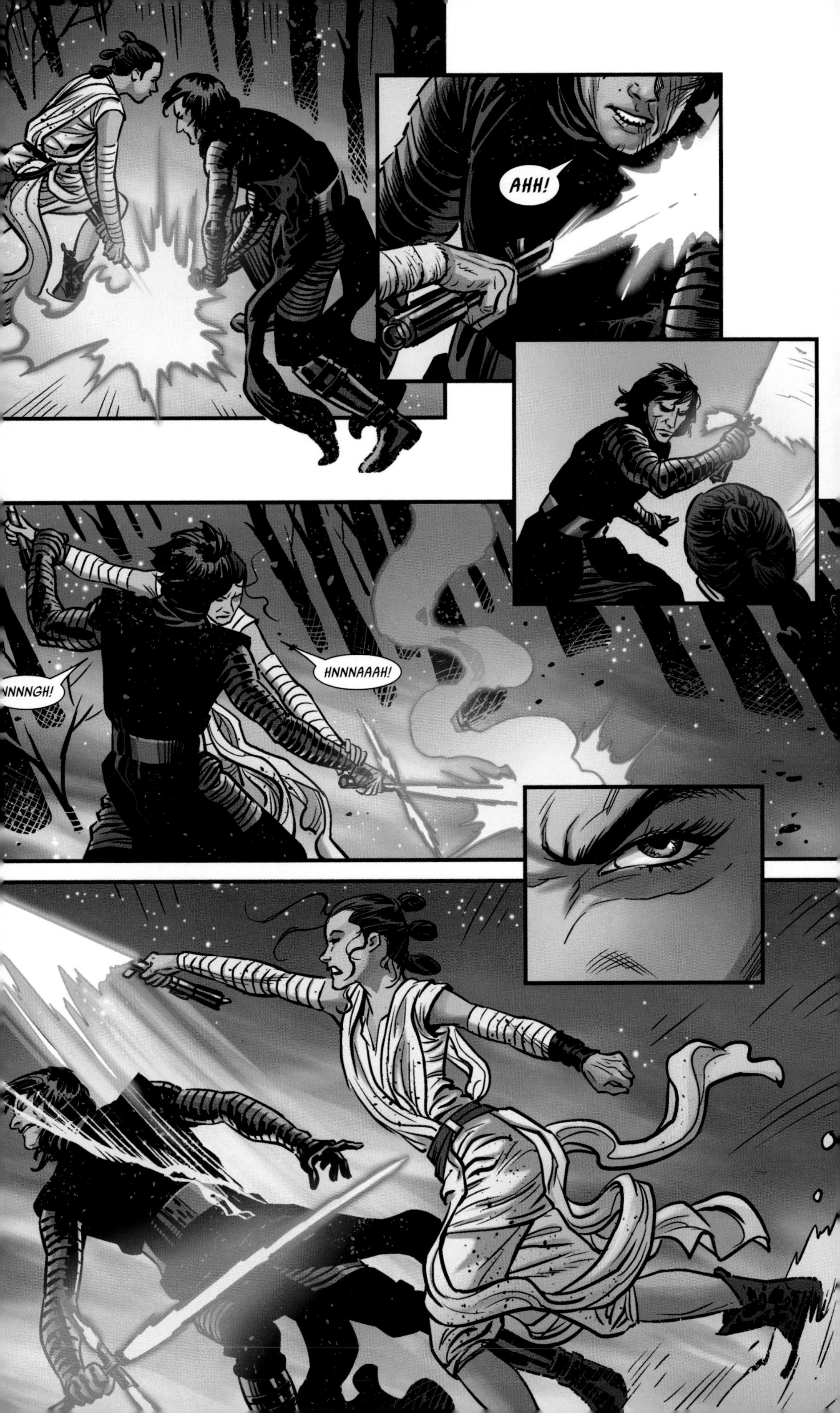
AHH!
NNNNGH!
HNNNAAAH!

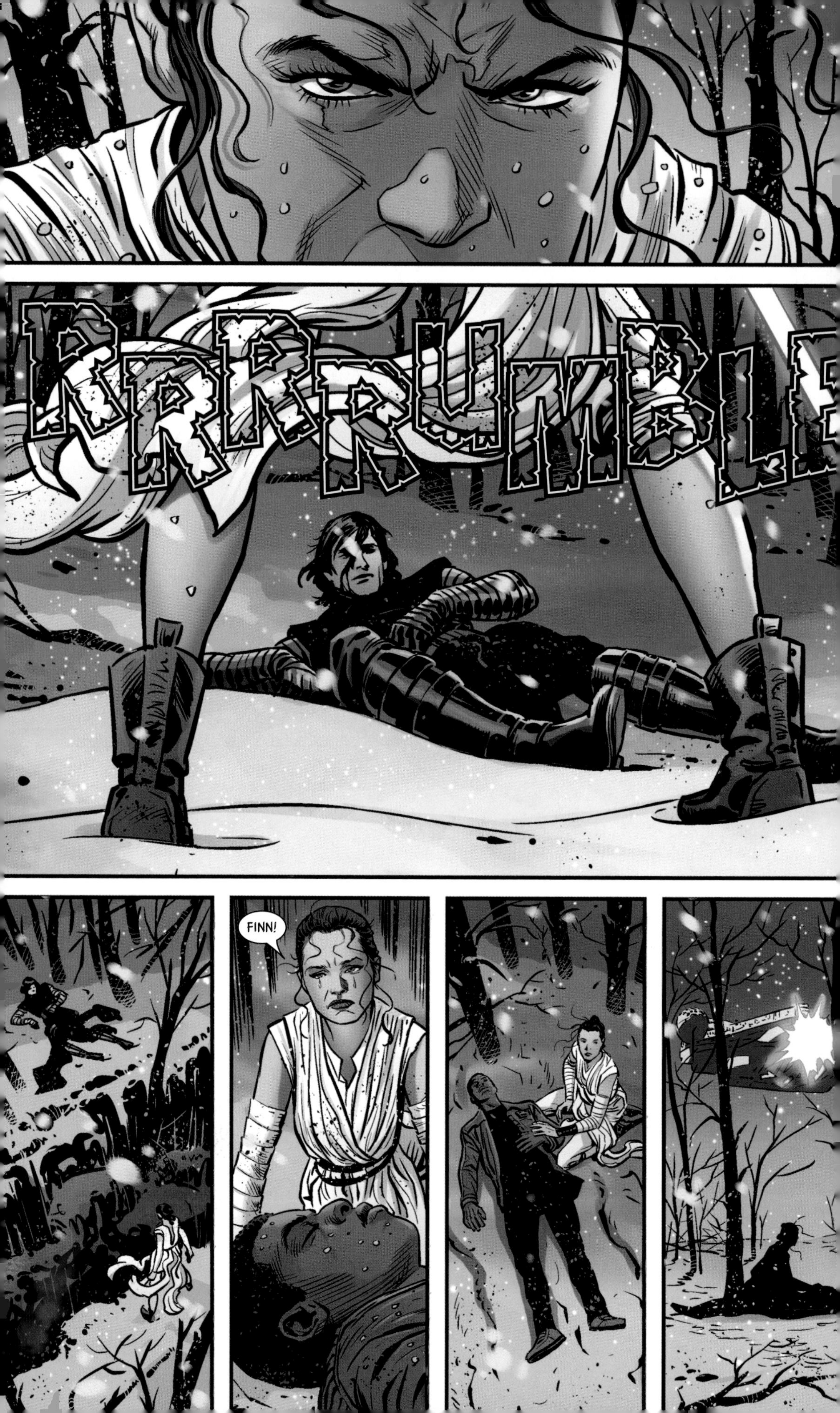
KRRRRUMBLE
FINN!

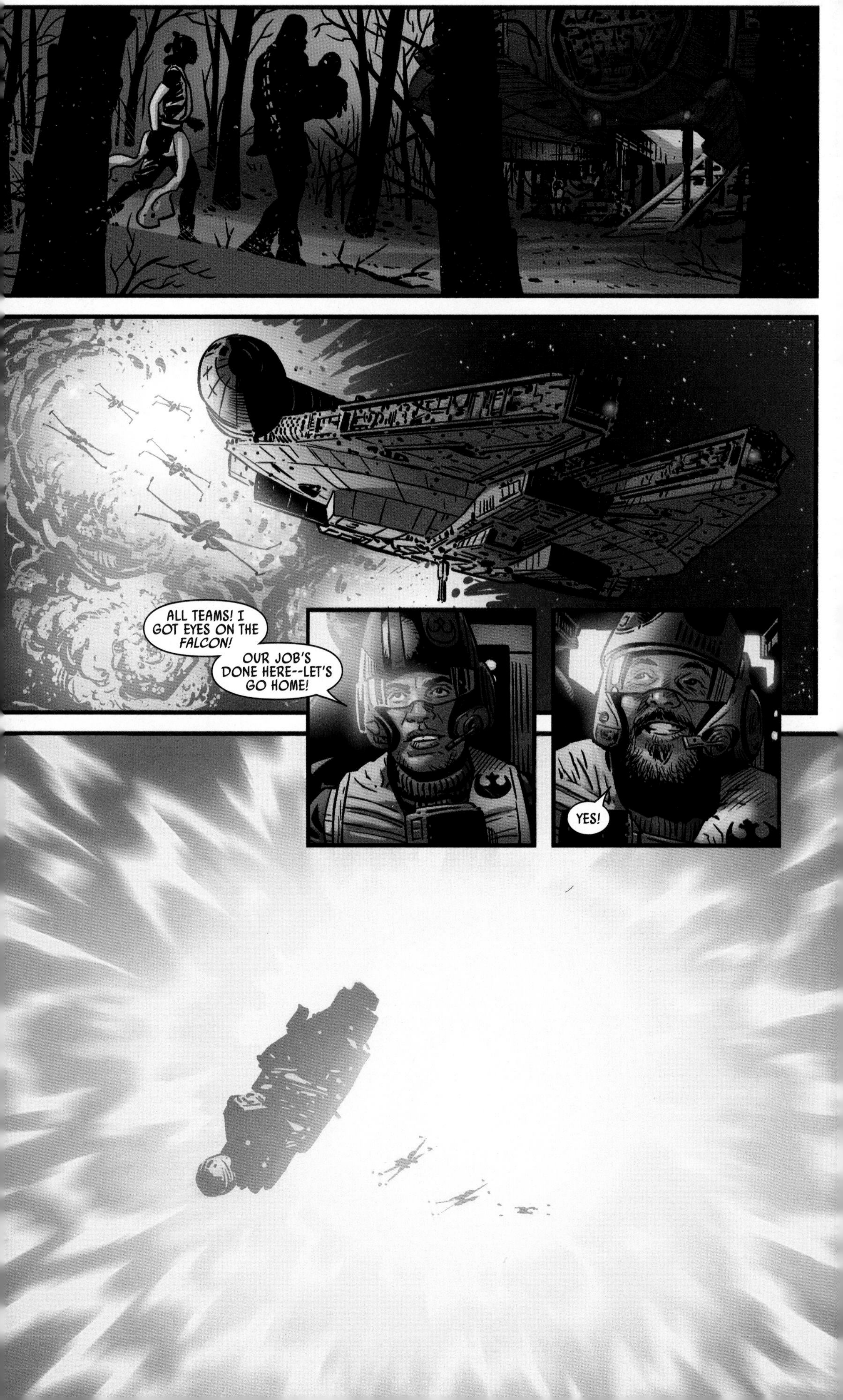
ALL TEAMS! I GOT EYES ON THE FALCON!
OUR JOB'S DONE HERE--LET'S GO HOME!
YES!

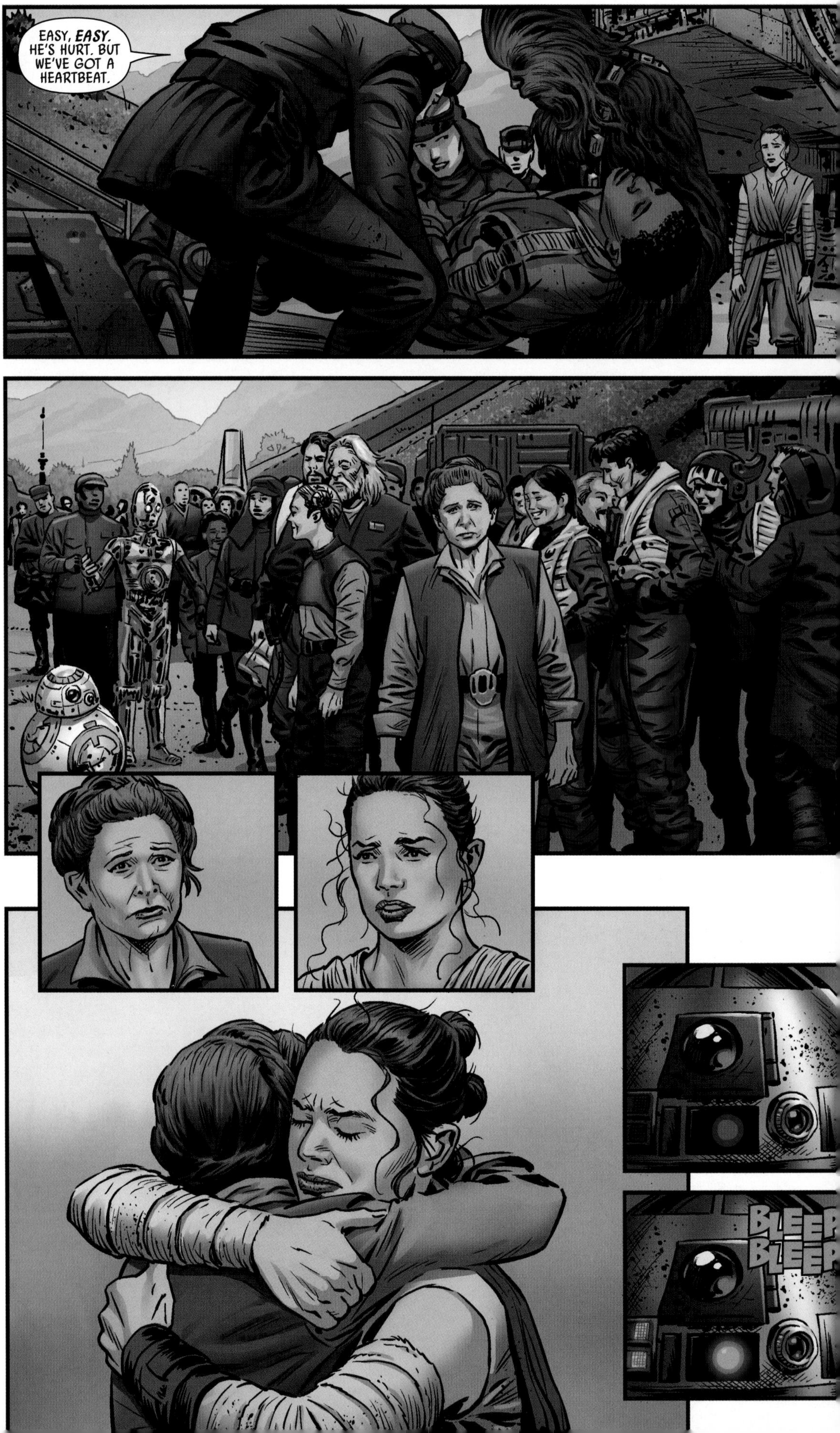
EASY, *EASY*. HE'S HURT. BUT WE'VE GOT A HEARTBEAT.

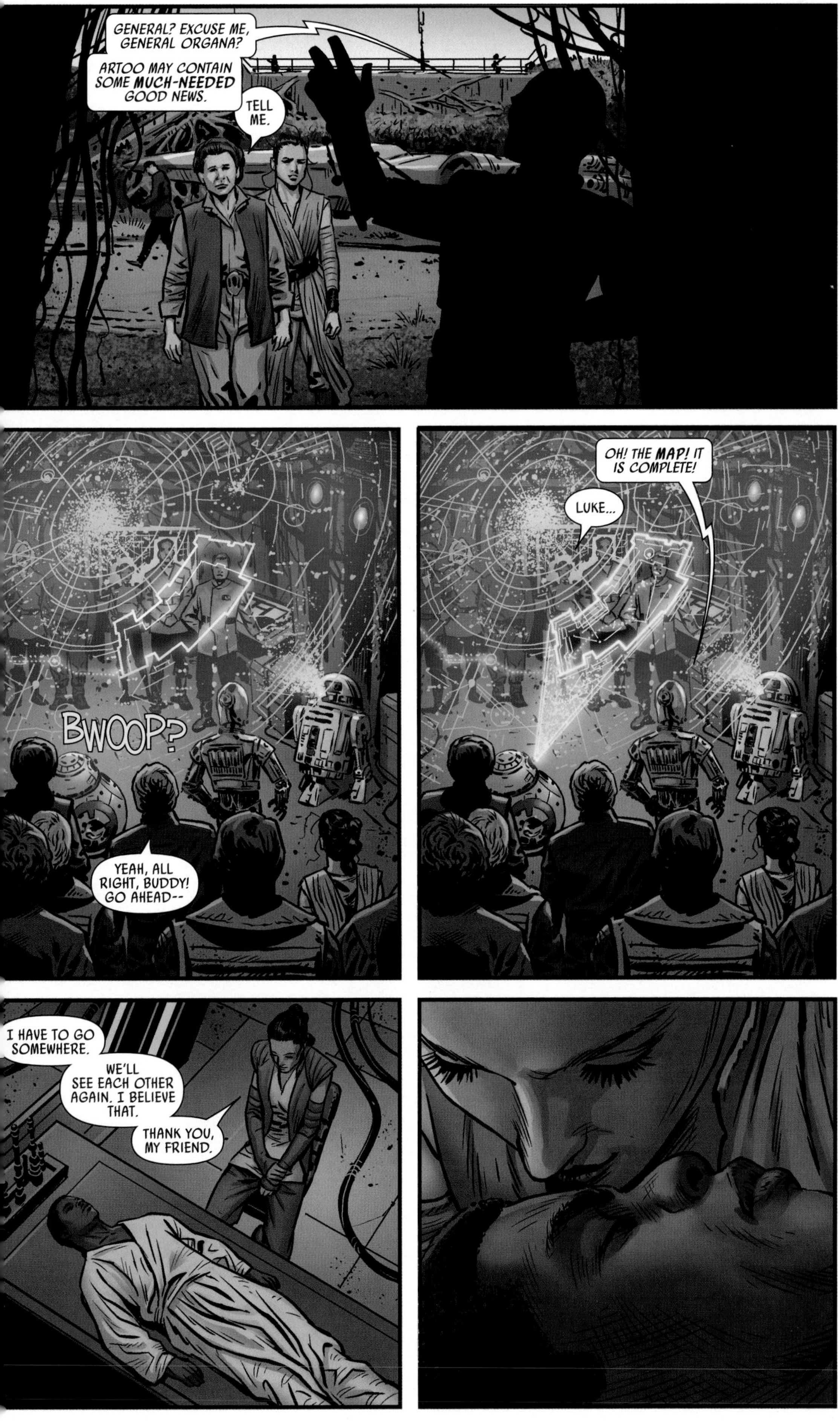
GENERAL? EXCUSE ME, GENERAL ORGANA?
ARTOO MAY CONTAIN SOME MUCH-NEEDED GOOD NEWS.
TELL ME.
BWOOP?
YEAH, ALL RIGHT, BUDDY! GO AHEAD--
OH! THE MAP! IT IS COMPLETE!
LUKE...
I HAVE TO GO SOMEWHERE.
WE'LL SEE EACH OTHER AGAIN. I BELIEVE THAT.
THANK YOU, MY FRIEND.

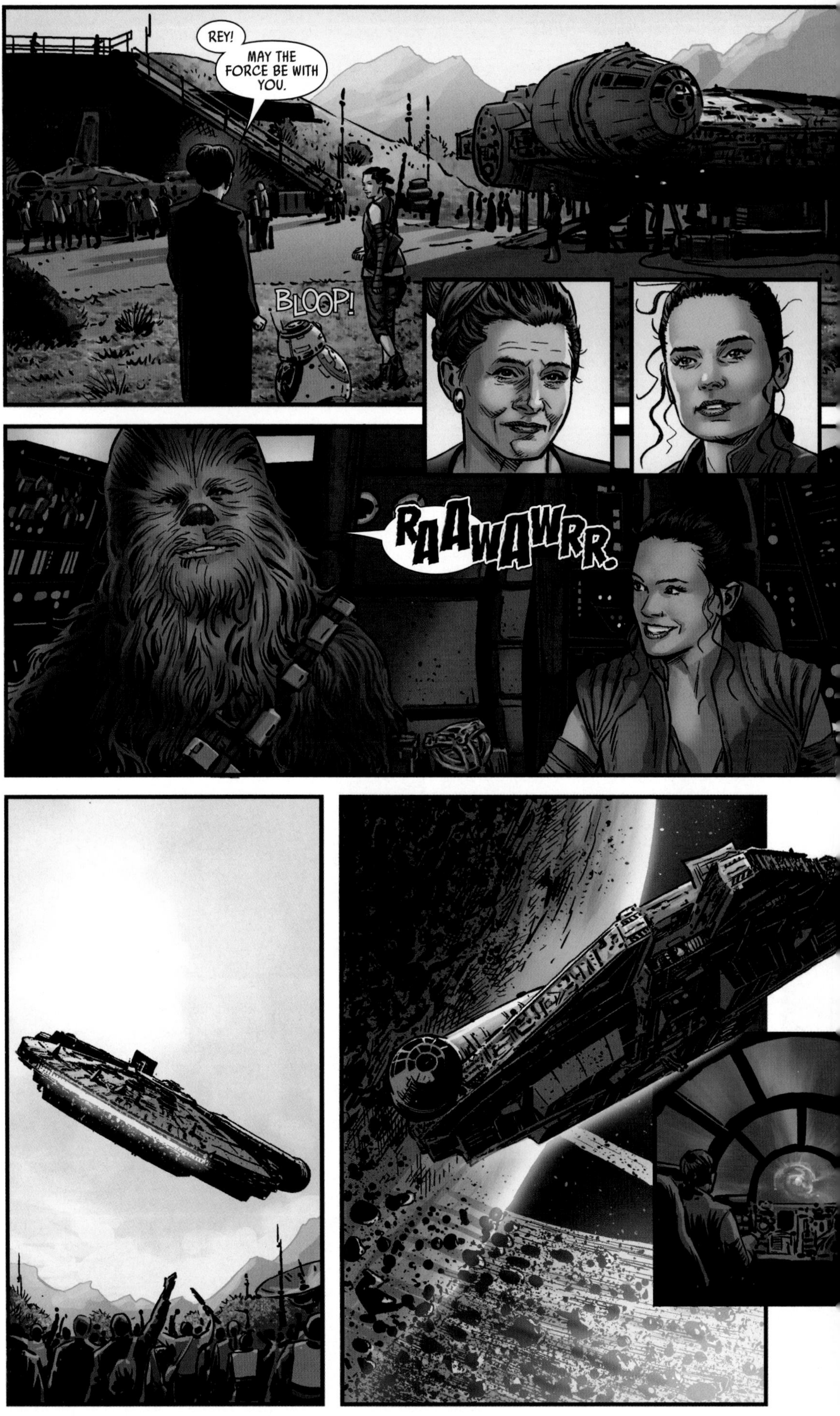
REY!
MAY THE FORCE BE WITH YOU.
BLOOP!
RAAWAWRR.

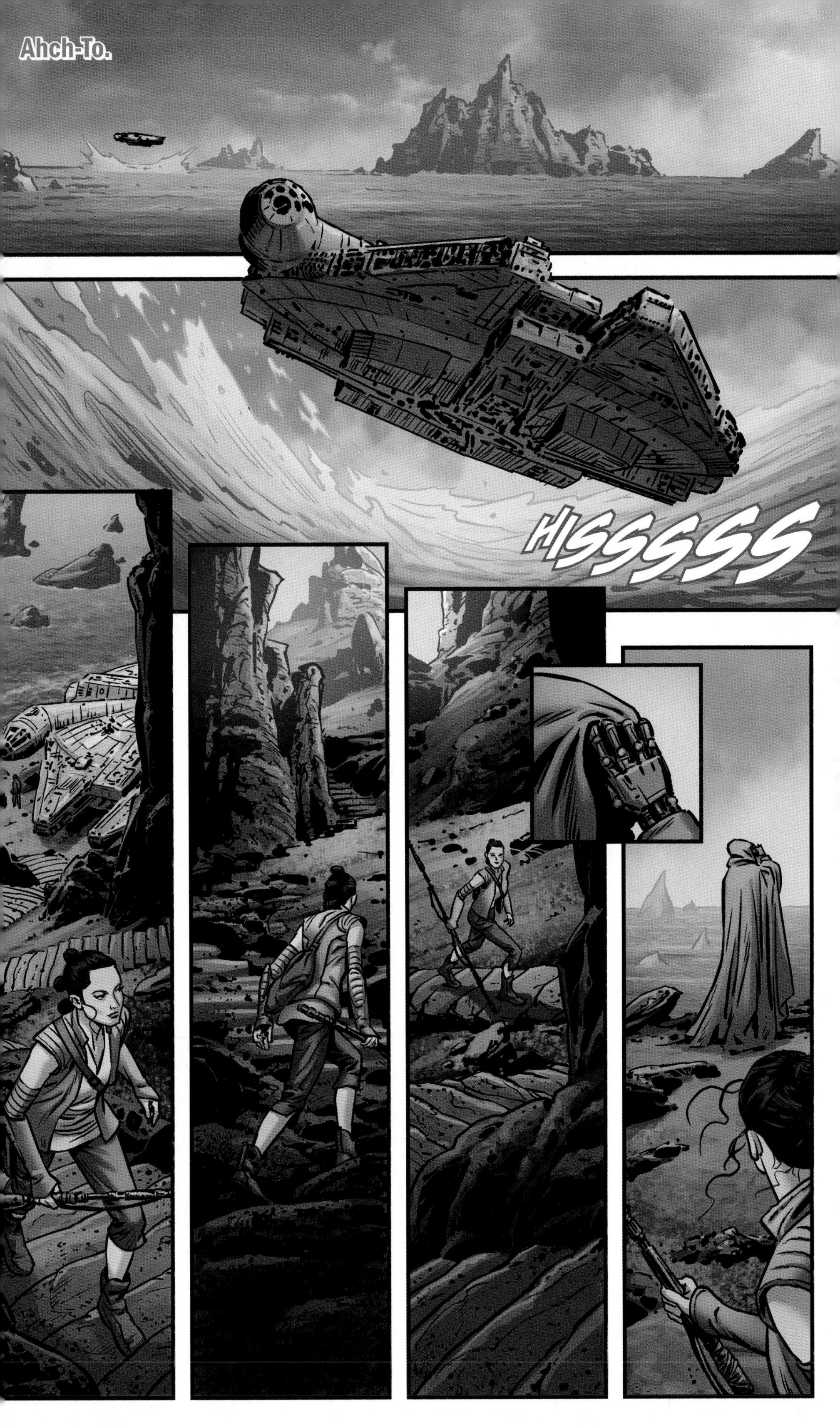
Ahch-To.
HISSSSS

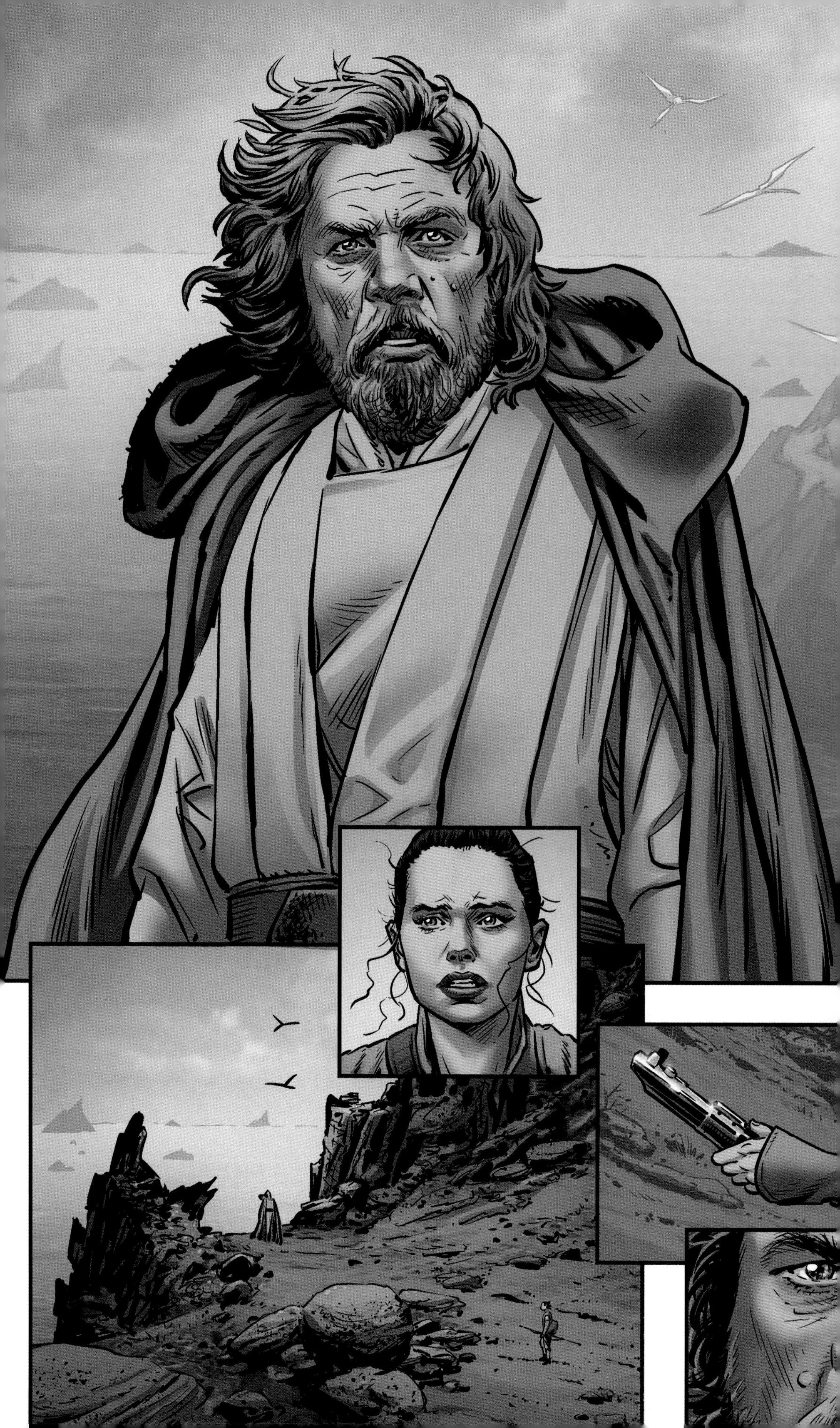